WELCOME TO

Beast Quest

Collect the special coins in this book.
You will earn one gold coin for
every chapter you read.

Once you have finished all the chapters,
find out what to do with your gold coins at
the back of the book.

With special thanks to Tabitha Jones

For Susan and Martin Eley

www.beastquest.co.uk

ORCHARD BOOKS

First published in Great Britain in 2016 by The Watts Publishing Group

1 3 5 7 9 10 8 6 4 2

Text © 2016 Beast Quest Limited.
Cover and inside illustrations by Steve Sims
© Beast Quest Limited 2016

Beast Quest is a registered trademark of Beast Quest Limited
Series created by Beast Quest Limited, London

A CIP catalogue record for this book is available from the British Library.

ISBN 978 1 40834 088 2

Printed and bound by CPI Group (UK) Ltd, Croydon, CR0 4YY

The paper and board used in this book are made from wood from responsible sources

Orchard Books
An imprint of Hachette Children's Group
Part of The Watts Publishing Group Limited
Carmelite House, 50 Victoria Embankment, London EC4Y 0DZ

An Hachette UK Company
www.hachette.co.uk
www.hachettechildrens.co.uk

Soara
the Stinging
Spectre

BY ADAM BLADE

ORCHARD

VILLAGE

KING
HUGO'S
PALACE

KARIXA'S MINE

TRIAL OF HEROES

JUNGLE

CORSAIR ISLAND

CONTENTS

A great battle has just taken place in Avantia. The City was almost destroyed by a raging Beast, and many lives were at risk...

Thankfully, a courageous warrior came to our aid, and peace was restored to the capital. But this warrior was not Tom, nor was it Elenna, for they were across the ocean, fighting bravely on another Quest. Now Avantia has a new champion, laying claim to Tom's title of Master of the Beasts.

And this courageous fighter has an honest claim to that title, which means there is only one thing for it.

Tom must put his title on the line. He and his opponent must complete the Trial of Heroes.

May the bravest warrior win.

Aduro, former wizard to King Hugo

THE OTHER SIDE OF THE ABYSS

Tom fell through silence, a thick, heavy nothingness pressing in on him from every side. He strained to see something – anything – but the blackness was so complete he might as well have been blind.

Then the opposite – white light flooding his vision. Tom threw

up an arm to shield his eyes and
blinked, struggling to focus in the
sudden brightness. And, once he
could, he found himself standing
on a deserted beach gazing out at a
perfectly clear sea. A moment later,
Elenna stumbled to his side.

She shuddered, as if shaking away
the touch of the abyss, then squinted
into the glaring sun. "What is this
place?" she asked.

Tom shrugged. He'd never seen
anywhere like it. Powdery grey sand
stretched away on either side and
led down to the water's edge. The
sea was still and silent, its smooth
surface as transparent as glass. Lilac
clouds scudded across a purple sky

above them at an impossible speed, but Tom couldn't feel the faintest breeze on his skin.

"I think we've reached stage two of the Trial of Heroes," he said.

"Hey! Stop gawking and get out of my way!" a female voice blurted behind them. "I've got a Beast to kill!" Elbows shoved Tom and Elenna aside and Amelia barged past, closely followed by Dray, her silent, hulking uncle.

Amelia put her hands on her hips and gazed out at the strange, flat landscape. "So, I guess it's a race to the next Beast, then," she said, her blustery tone tinged with unease.

About time she began to realise

this isn't a game! Tom thought.

Amelia drew a compass from her pocket and turned her back, blocking Tom and Elenna's view of the device.

Tom clenched his teeth. "If you don't want to get disqualified for cheating," he said, "you'd better let us all use that compass."

Amelia's broad shoulders tensed and Tom knew he'd hit a nerve. Despite all Tom had done for Avantia, as a direct descendent of Kara the Fearless, Amelia had as much right to the title of Master of the Beasts as he did. Tom had given up his jewelled belt and magical armour when he'd agreed to undertake the Trial of Heroes, on which two rivals raced to find the mythical Rune of Courage in an enchanted realm called the Nowhere Lands. By the rules of the trial, Amelia should have brought no magical artefacts either, but she had somehow managed to sneak out with Tom's compass.

Amelia shrugged and turned. "Fine," she said, holding the compass out before her. "It won't make any difference – I'll still win because I'm the rightful Mistress of the Beasts."

Tom and Elenna exchanged an exasperated look, then craned over the compass in Amelia's hand. Amelia moved the compass slowly over the landscape, pointing first along the empty beach to their left. The compass needle didn't so much as twitch. Amelia turned,

and Tom and Elenna turned with
her, watching the compass closely
as Amelia ran it along the beach to
their right. Still nothing. Finally,
Amelia turned to face the motionless
sea. She held the compass towards
a small, steep-sided island carpeted
with dark green, lush vegetation.
A narrow grey beach ringed the
island's forested cliffs. The compass
needle swung slowly between
Destiny and *Danger*. Amelia stopped,
frowning at the island.

"It looks like we need to get out
there somehow," Elenna said.

"I wouldn't recommend it." A voice
like a rusty hinge spoke from
behind them.

Tom turned to see a lean, bow-legged woman grinning at him from a wrinkled, sun-browned face. Skinny arms and legs stuck like knobbly twigs from the woman's woven grass tunic, and a halo of white hair stood out from her head. Bracelets threaded with what looked like the delicate bones of small birds decorated her wrists and ankles, and she carried a long bone spear. One of her pupils was misted white but her eyes glittered as they scanned Tom's face.

"You think it's a bad idea?" Tom said.

The old woman's gap-toothed grin broadened and she lifted her hands, the gnarled fingers curled like claws. "The strange ones live there," she said, eyes swivelling madly. "They don't like visitors." She dropped her hands, and shrugged. "Why not stay here instead? I'll make you some tea."

Tom shook his head, wondering if this woman was part of the trial – a way to stop them succeeding. "I'm afraid we have to get to that island." He glanced again at the forested cliffs, worry gnawing at his belly. *The strange ones? Could they be in league with the Beast?* Elenna shot him an uneasy look.

"I'm not afraid of a few islanders," Amelia said, hefting her axe. The old woman chuckled.

"Is that so?" she said. "That must be nice for you. But only a fool lives without fear."

Amelia scowled and balled a fist. "Who are you, anyway?" she barked.

Tom quickly stepped between her and the old woman. "Do you know a way to the island?" he asked.

At the same moment, Elenna nudged him and pointed. A wooden dinghy, almost the same bleached grey as the sand, rested near the tideline. The old woman followed the line of Elenna's pointed finger.

"Might we borrow that boat?" Tom asked. The woman shrugged again.

"The boat belongs to no one. A brave young warrior tried to reach

the island a long time ago, but only the
boat came back." The woman lifted her
hands again, her eyes wide with mock
horror. "I reckon the strange ones got

him!" She let out a long, delighted cackle, then suddenly turned and hobbled away, her feet leaving barely a trace in the sand.

"She's a pretty strange one herself if you ask me," Amelia muttered. "Come on, Uncle!" She gestured to Dray who stood nearby, as still and silent as a tree. "Beast number two is waiting!" The huge man lurched after Amelia as she marched towards the boat.

Elenna gazed at the island, gnawing her lip. "It sounds like the last hero to take the trial never made it home," she said.

Tom nodded. The eerie, bruise-coloured landscape filled him

with dread, setting all his senses
thrumming. "You're right," he said.
"And he didn't have to babysit
Amelia-the-reckless and her lump of
an uncle. We'll have to keep our wits
about us if we're going to get us all
out of here alive."

He was trying to sound confident,
but the truth was that Amelia had
already proved herself brave, if a
little foolhardy. He wasn't planning
on letting her win the title, but he
didn't want her to come to serious
harm either.

Tom and Elenna hurried over the
sand, reaching the boat just after
Amelia and Dray. Patches of ancient-
looking silvery wood showed through

curls of flaking paint on the hull, but the inside looked sound and dry, with a narrow bench at each end. A pair of oars balanced in rowlocks either side of the prow. Amelia prodded the dinghy with her toe.

"There's no way that old thing will carry us all," she said.

"Then you'd better wait here," Tom said, pushing past her. He grabbed one side of the boat. Elenna took the other, and together they hauled the dinghy into the shallows. Even through his thick leather boots, Tom could feel that the water was ice-cold. The boat jerked in his hands, and he turned to see Amelia clambering aboard. Dray lumbered in after her, making the boat pitch violently.

"Let's go!" Amelia said.

Tom gave the dinghy a final shove, then leapt aboard. Amelia and Dray settled themselves side by side on the bench at the stern, leaving Tom and Elenna the narrower bench at the prow. They squeezed into their seat, and each took an oar.

Ripples drifted out over the glassy water as they rowed, and the steady splosh of their oars was the only sound to break the silence. The strange purple sky reflected in the water – tattered shadows mirroring the racing clouds above. Tom lifted his eyes to the dense greenery of the island in

the distance. Nothing stirred.

Then, suddenly, the water ahead bulged, rising up into a huge, crystal-clear swell. Elenna gasped as the rush of tumbling water filled the air.

"A tidal wave!" Amelia cried.

The impossible torrent forged
towards them, climbing higher
and higher.

2

THE SWARM

"Hang on tight!" Tom shouted, the deafening roar of the water almost swallowing his voice. He dipped his head, bracing himself... *Whoa!* Tom's heart leapt. Their tiny boat lurched skywards, caught up by the colossal wave. Tom clung tight to the dinghy side. He could feel the force of the raging water shuddering through the wood. Beside him, Elenna stared ahead, wide eyed with horror as the dinghy carried them higher, rising on the swell. A gaping trough of water opened up before them...

Crash! Tom's stomach fell away as they plunged into the wave's wake. Icy spray pummelled him, snatching his breath from his throat, drenching his hair and clothes.

"Agh!" Amelia screamed. Tom turned to see her flailing in the water, one hand on the stern, her legs tugged out behind her by the sucking sea. Dray merely clung to his seat, making no move to help her.

"Grab my hand!" Tom cried, leaning towards Amelia, stretching as far as he could. She reached, folding his palm in a powerful grip. Tom braced himself against her weight. At the same moment, Amelia yanked his arm, pulling herself into the boat. The force of Amelia's tug ripped Tom's hand from the dinghy side and sent him careering headfirst towards the churning water.

"Tom!" he heard Elenna cry.

But her voice was lost in a rush of water as he plunged below the waves. Tom's flesh shrank from the biting cold and his muscles locked. He clamped his jaws shut against the deadly urge to gasp. Bubbles whooshed past his face and the grey seabed sped up to meet him. The sucking current dragged him down, and he pumped his arms and legs, trying to right himself.

Tom heard a muffled splash above and looked up to see Dray sinking through the water, surrounded by a glittering cloud of bubbles. *He's fallen in too!* The big man's eyes were wide, staring at something behind Tom. Tom spun. Silver-blue fish filled his view, knifing towards him. Sharp triangular fins jutted from their spines, and beneath their glassy, staring eyes, long narrow bills tapered to deadly points.

Swordfish! Tom realised. *And they're swarming us – just like the bats on the last stage of the trial!*

Tom kicked with all his might
towards the bright surface. His wet
clothes dragged at his arms and legs,

and his shield weighed him down.
Dray swam just ahead, his long arms
and legs propelling him through the
water. Tom's lungs throbbed, but he
powered after the giant man, and
finally broke the surface. He sucked
in a dizzying gulp of air, desperately
treading water to keep his head
above the violent swell. Dray's bald
head bobbed in the water nearby,
surrounded by sharp triangular fins.

Ahead, Elenna and Amelia rowed
frantically towards them, the dinghy
rising and falling on the tumbling
waves. But it wasn't getting any
closer.

Ow! Tom felt a sharp point jab his
thigh. He glanced down to see at least

ten hollow-eyed swordfish staring up at him. Then, in a frenzy of thrashing silver flesh, they all attacked at once. Bills snickered right and left, lashing at Tom's clothes and skin.

Dray let out a roar of anger and Tom saw a bloodless gash on the man's cheek where a fish had struck him. Tom lifted his sword and used the flat of the blade to bat the stabbing bills aside – but there were so many, and his movements were slow and clumsy in his waterlogged clothes. They prodded him again and again until the water around him was pink with his own blood.

Dray pummelled the swordfish with his massive fists, while the sea churned with more glossy silver bodies.

"I'm coming, Tom!" Elenna cried, her jaw set as she rowed with all her strength. Amelia grimaced with effort, pushing her oar through the unnatural waves.

The boat inched closer, its progress painfully slow. Tom struggled and gasped, fighting to stay afloat while thrusting and batting with his sword. His body stung in dozens of places from the fishes' cruel jabs. Finally, Tom kicked to meet the boat, pushing between muscular, scaled bodies and slashing blades. Relief flooded through him as he managed to grab hold of it. He dropped his sword inside.

Suddenly, Dray's huge form shouldered Tom aside, ripping his fingers from the wood. "Hey!" Tom

cried, bristling with anger. Dray hauled himself aboard and Tom reached again for the dinghy. But, before he could grab it, something snagged his leg, pulling him below the waves, in among the slashing swordfish. He didn't have time to take a breath, and pumped his arms and kicked, panic building, his chest throbbing with lack of air. He couldn't free his leg!

Through the raging water and stabbing fish, Tom saw Elenna's pale hand reach down towards him. He grabbed it and she pulled him up towards the boat.

Tom broke the surface. Straining all his muscles, he managed to haul himself in beside Elenna, dragging a huge fish with him, its sharp sword snagged on the fabric of his trouser-leg.

The great fish flopped and writhed, its mouth gaping and its eyes rolling.

Amelia drew back her axe. "I'll deal with it!" she cried.

"No!" Elenna pushed her back. "Don't kill it!"

Tom's fingers fumbled with the creature's bill, tugging it from the fabric of his trouser-leg. As soon as it was free, the swordfish flexed its giant body and flipped back into the waves. A moment later, it dived after the rest of the shoal, now speeding away from the boat.

"Why do you think they gave up?"
Tom asked, watching the fishes'
sharp dorsal fins cutting through
the swell.

"I think that might have something

to do with it!" Elenna said.

Tom turned to see her pointing at something rising through the choppy water... Something that made his stomach clench with fear.

3

DEAD BLOOD

It was a vast, bloated balloon of colourless gelatinous flesh, trailing hundreds of straggling tentacles tipped with toothy barbs – a jellyfish. But its domed body looked as wide as the main square back in Tom's home village, Errinel. Embedded deep within its transparent flesh Tom could see broken beams of wood, pale bones,

and even what looked like a whole
sailing ship, complete with rigging
and sails.

"What is that thing?" Amelia said,
her voice quavering with fear.

"The Beast, clearly!" Elenna said,

already fumbling for her oar.

Tom couldn't take his eyes off
the monstrous creature. The top
of its body broke the surface and
water poured from its transparent
flesh. A dimple formed in the jelly,

widening and deepening, until, like water spiralling down a drain, a gaping whirlpool opened up in the monster's giant back. The sea around the creature swirled, sucked into the eddy of flesh, and the dinghy lurched, caught up in the violent current. A shock of adrenaline jolted Tom into action. He lifted his sword.

"We have to fight!" he cried. "That thing's going to suck us in!" Tom staggered and almost fell as the dinghy lurched sideways towards the monstrous jellyfish. "Elenna, Dray – you row! Keep us from being sucked in," he cried. "Amelia! We have to fight that thing together, or we're all dead." Amelia's mouth opened and shut as she stared wide-eyed at the sucking, swirling mass of jelly beside them. Then she shook herself, and lifted her axe. Dray grunted, rowing hard with long strokes on the opposite side of the boat from the Beast. Elenna dipped her oar again and again into the spiralling water.

The boat pitched crazily from side to side, dragged towards the giant jellyfish. Tom scanned the bulging, slimy body of the hideous creature, looking for a weak spot to strike. He spread his feet wide and bent his knees for balance, then leaned over the side of the rocking boat.

The putrid stench of decaying fish rose in waves off the shiny dome of the Beast's body. Deep inside, Tom could see the sailing ship clearly now, ragged sails for ever still, trapped like an insect in amber. He sliced down at the clear flesh with his sword. It parted easily with a flare of blue light, then rippled back together, the gash closing with a sickening slurp. Tom slashed again, and Amelia hacked at the monster with her axe, sending a gobbet of glowing jelly flying. But, every cut they made slapped closed with a sucking pop, releasing more rancid, choking gas.

"Die, curse you!" Amelia shouted,

chopping furiously at the monster's vast body. Her axe plunged into the soft, yielding jelly and lodged there.

"Hey!" Amelia cried, yanking at her axe, but its head sank deeper

into the flesh, jerking her forwards. She braced her knees against the gunwale and tugged, her face red and her body trembling with the effort. "No. You. Don't!" she roared. But her fingers were almost brushing the creature's body, and the boat was listing horribly. Tom leaned over as far as he could and plunged the blade of his sword deep into the soft, putrid flesh. *Clang!* He knocked the axe head free. Amelia fell backwards into the boat as the creature's wound healed with a wet slap.

"Put your back into it, you two!" Amelia barked at Dray and Elenna. "It's time to get out of here!"

Dray's fierce grimace deepened

and he rowed faster. Beside Dray, Elenna's breath came in harsh rasps as she worked to keep up. Tom sank down and plunged his sword into the water, using the flat of the blade to push against the whirling current. Beside him, Amelia rowed with her axe. Waves battered at the little boat and Tom's arm burned with every stroke, but they started to break away from the whirlpool surrounding the vile mound of flesh. They edged towards the island, gaining speed.

"Keep going!" Tom cried. "We're going to make it!" But at the same moment, a slender tendril lashed past him, sending a spray of

water into his eyes.

"Ah!" Elenna screamed. Tom cleared his eyes to see the tendril whip away, leaving a bright red cut on Elenna's forearm.

"We have to get to that island!"

she said, her voice suddenly wild with panic. Tom could see her stroke faltering and the colour draining from her cheeks. Behind them, the vast jellyfish let out a rumbling belch and sank below the waves. Tom grabbed Elenna's oar. She slumped into the boat, clutching her arm. Tom drove his oar again and again through the water. He glanced back to see the jellyfish shoot away across the seabed, its glimmering tentacles trailing.

"Ha! We scared it away!" Amelia said.

"It'll be back," Tom said. "And we'll have to defeat it." On the floor of the boat, Elenna gritted her teeth, bent double over her injured arm. *She's badly hurt*, thought Tom.

"Quickly!" he said. The seabed rose beneath them towards the narrow beach that surrounded the forested island. A little to the right, Tom spotted an inlet, funnelling through the cliffs. "That way!" he cried, pointing.

Tom, Dray and Amelia rowed together, hard and fast through the inlet. Lush greenery sprouted from the steep cliffs either side, overshadowing their boat with huge dark leaves. Finally, the cliffs dropped away, and the inlet opened out into a wide sandy cove. Steeply rising forested slopes formed a

circular basin around the cove – all
that was left of an ancient volcano,
now smothered with mosses, ferns
and dense bushes with waxy leaves.

As they neared the beach, Tom leapt from the boat. "Help me," he told Amelia.

"Go on, Dray!" Amelia said, keeping her seat.

The silent man plunged knee-deep into the crystal sea and grabbed the other side of the dinghy. Tom and Dray hauled together, dragging the boat onto the sand. Amelia leapt out, and Tom gave Elenna his hand. She stepped shakily from the dinghy, then stumbled. Tom dipped his shoulder under her arm and hurried her towards a mossy rock, half buried in grass.

Elenna slumped against the rock. Tom gasped – the red cut across her arm had turned almost purple, and Tom could clearly see the veins standing out black against her pale skin.

"Dead blood," Elenna said weakly. She lifted her eyes to Tom's face, and they were filled with terror. "The jellyfish poisoned me with its sting," she said. "My uncle warned me of this when we fished together. My blood…" She shuddered violently. "It's rotting in my veins."

4

PIRANHA PIRATES

Tom felt sick. "There has to be a cure!"

Elenna nodded. "Sanguin root." She tried to rise, glancing frantically at the plants all around her, but then grimaced and fell back. "It's a herb with blood-red leaves," she said. "If there's some on the island, I stand a chance. Otherwise—" Elenna's eyes suddenly rolled upwards. Her body sagged and her eyes flickered closed.

"Elenna!" Tom cried, shaking her shoulder, but she didn't stir.

Tom's guts churned with horror.

"We have to find sanguin root!" Tom cried, turning to find Amelia right behind him.

"You mean, *you* do!" Amelia said. "Come on, Uncle! This is our chance!"

Dray obeyed, pushing the dinghy back into the deeper water, then climbing aboard himself.

"Are you mad?" Tom shouted.

Amelia glowered back at him over her shoulder. "Cowards never triumph!" she said.

"Elenna might die!" Tom cried. "And without us, you don't stand a chance!"

Tom saw a flicker of uncertainly cross Amelia's face. She sat upright,

frowning back at him as Dray
continued to row. Then she hitched
her chin. "You'll find the herb with or
without us!" she said. "I'm not afraid.
It's my destiny to be Mistress of the
Beasts!" Amelia turned back to her
rowing.

Tom fought the urge to run into the
shallows after them. He had to help
Elenna. He turned to see his friend
lying in the grass beside the rock,
her chest rising and falling with fast,
shallow breaths. The sight of the
black lines creeping up her arm filled
him with dread.

"I'll find that root," he whispered in
her ear. "I promise!"

Beyond the sandy beach of the cove,

a tangle of dense vegetation covered the basin sides. Tom raced into the undergrowth. Tall palm trees rose high above his head and coarse grass snagged at his feet as he climbed. Bushes with dark glossy leaves and bright flowers blocked his path, but he pushed past, scanning the ground for any trace of red. The air was humid and heavy with the pungent scent of bruised greenery and sickly sweet flowers. Tom's tunic soon stuck to his back with sweat. He spotted every shade of green and gold, huge flowers in rich purples and pinks, dark, twisted trunks and black rocks...

But nothing red!

He slashed at branches with his sword, breaking through the tangled plants pressed close around him. His breath rasped in his throat and his skin prickled with sweat. Panic squeezed his chest every time he thought of Elenna back on the beach, her blood rotting in her veins, running out of time. Finally, wild horror took hold of him. He picked up his pace, stumbling onwards, almost falling on gnarled roots as he scanned the foliage all around him, his fierce determination giving way to fury and hopelessness.

I failed, he thought, his limbs heavy with dread. *Elenna's going to die!* But then he spotted a flash of bright red through a thicket of lacy ferns. His heart swelled and a surge of energy pushed him onwards, through the matted, grasping leaves...

But the bright red was not a herb or even a flower.

It was a pair of bulging eyes, set in a dark, scaled face. Tom's flesh crawled at the sight of the creature's jutting lower jaw and gaping mouth, crowded with sharp, triangular teeth. The face was that of a piranha, but it poked from the ruffled neckline of a grimy shirt, perched on the broad, muscular body of a man holding a gleaming cutlass.

A piranha pirate? They must be

*what the old woman was speaking
of when she mentioned the
strange ones.*

Tom reeled back as two more,
shorter creatures, dressed in leather
breeches and waistcoats and with

the same, gaping fishy faces,
crashed out of the forest. Each had
a stout red stick jutting from his
belt, with a length of twisted string
at one end.

Dynamite!

Tom stared in disbelief at the three nightmarish figures. All stood taller than he did in knee-high boots, their broad, barrel chests puffed out before them, their red eyes watching him keenly. One of the two smaller pirates wore a tatty bandana over one eye, just showing the edge of a jagged scar. The other had a wooden stump sticking out from his frayed trouser leg in place of a boot.

"What's a puny soft-skin like you doing on Corsair Island?" the tallest of the creatures croaked, his throat bulging like a frog's as he made the words. "Soara the Stinging Spectre should have made short work of such a skinny sprat. How did you get past her?"

Tom guessed that Soara was the name of the jellyfish-Beast. He chose his words carefully.

"I came across the sea in a small boat," Tom said, "but my friend was poisoned by Soara. I wish you no harm, only friendship, but I must find a blood-red herb called sanguin root, or my friend will die. Do you know of such a herb?"

The three piranha men looked at each other, their toothy mouths widening into what looked like horrible smirks.

The tallest finally turned back to Tom, an odd smirk on his fishy

face. "Aye," he said. "We know where it grows. But nothing comes free on Corsair Island." He lifted his cutlass, and shifted his weight into an unmistakable fighting stance. "If you want the plant, you'll have to best me!"

5

DUEL

With no choice, Tom lifted his sword, sizing up the huge, muscled fish-man leering back at him. *This Quest is getting weirder by the moment,* he thought. *But I have to save Elenna...*

He squared his shoulders. "I'm ready for you!" he said. But at the same moment, the pirate with the bandana dipped his head and

charged. Tom lifted his shield to
block the attack but the broad,
scaled head smashed it aside and
cannoned onwards, striking Tom
hard in the gut. The force of the blow

bowled him over, sending his sword and shield flying.

Tom scrabbled in the dirt for his weapon, but a pair of strong hands gripped his ankles and hefted him up. Dark greenery whirled past Tom as he was spun around and around, then sent flying, into the muscled arms of the biggest pirate. The huge fish-man plonked him back on his feet. When Tom's head stopped spinning, he found himself facing the smaller pirate with the bandana. The scarred fish-man glared back at Tom from his single bulging eye. He snapped his toothy jaws. Then, with a quick flex of his stubby neck, the pirate lifted his fists and started to bounce from foot to foot, his knees bent and his elbows tight to his sides.

A boxing match? Tom's mouth went dry. The piranha pirate had to be twice his weight at least.

"Now fight!" the lead pirate croaked from behind him.

Tom lifted his own fists, his body poised on the balls of his feet. The pirate twitched his broad shoulders and made a couple of warning jabs, then lunged, his meaty fist ploughing towards Tom's temple. Tom ducked, then leapt sideways, narrowly missing a savage uppercut to the chin.

The creature stepped back and

scowled at Tom, then beckoned with his fingers. "Come on!" he said, in a low, husky voice.

Tom lunged, jabbing for the pirate's massive jaw. A broad forearm whipped up, blocking his punch, but Tom followed up with a right hook to the gut. *THUD!* Tom winced in pain as his fist connected with the creature's belly. It felt like he'd hit a brick wall. He danced back, slipping his head aside to avoid a fierce punch, then watched the big fish circle him, fists raised.

"Hurry up, Chomper!" the lead pirate growled from the sidelines. "Flatten the soft-skin!"

Chomper cricked his neck from

side to side with a horrible crunch,
then let out a snarl, his single red
eye never leaving Tom's face.

*With scales like that, I'll never
beat him in a fistfight!* Tom realised.
His hand still ached from the punch
he'd landed. Tom's sword gleamed
invitingly from the greenery just
beyond his bulky opponent. *He's
definitely strong, but I'm quicker!*
Tom threw himself forwards into
a roll past the pirate and snatched
up his sword. He was back on his
feet and behind the man before
his opponent could even turn.
Tom slipped his sword around the
pirate's thick neck, pressing the
blade into smooth glossy skin. The

pirate stiffened. Tom could see the pulse of blood through the thin membrane of the piranha's throat. He pressed his blade harder against the delicate flesh. "Do you yield?" Tom asked.

The pirate let out a low, furious

growl. Then he stamped his foot. "Aye!" he barked. Tom let his blade fall and stepped back. The pirate slunk away to join his companions, scowling at Tom all the while.

Tom's rush of victory quickly faded when the lead pirate stepped towards him and lifted his hefty cutlass. The huge blade, almost as long as Tom's leg, curved to a gleaming point.

"Time to fight fair, blade to blade," the pirate said. Something like laughter snorted from the creature's high, flat nostrils. Then, without warning, the pirate lunged, swinging the cutlass towards Tom's shoulder. Tom bent his arm and caught the

swipe on the flat of his sword,
then flicked his own blade down,
slicing at the creature's chest, just
below the armpit. His blade slid
harmlessly off the creature's scales.

"Yah!" The pirate's cutlass
plunged towards Tom's skull.

Tom threw up his weapon. *Clang!*
The shock of the blow jolted up
Tom's arm, numbing his hand
and almost buckling his elbow.
Somehow, he managed to hold his
sword steady. He looped it around
the piranha's blade and jabbed at
the man's barrel chest. His sword
pierced the creature's ruffled
shirt, but bounced off the flesh
underneath. Tom leapt back, his

sword arm smarting. The big pirate leered at him, his bulging eyes bright with amusement.

"Had enough?" he asked.

Tom lunged in answer, sending his blade slicing towards the pirate's chest. The pirate blocked and swung. Again and again their two swords clashed. Eager grunts and hisses rose from the watching piranha men. Again and again Tom made his way through the big pirate's defences, but each stab and thrust clashed harmlessly against tough scales. The creature's movements were clumsy and awkward, but he didn't seem to be tiring, while Tom's sword arm ached from blocking relentless blows, and his grip was slick with sweat. *I'm not going to win like this!* he realised, parrying a hefty thrust.

I need a stronger weapon... Then he had an idea. He shuffled back, letting the big pirate circle him. The pirate's crowded jaws twitched into a grin.

"Had enough now?" he asked again.

Tom leapt, kicking out hard, sending the soles of his boots slamming into the pirate's cutlass. The blade smashed into the big man's chest as Tom somersaulted backwards, landing on his feet. The pirate was staring open-mouthed at his hand, clamped to his chest, blood welling between the fingers where he'd been cut with his own sword. Tom sprinted past him, and turned, flicking his sword neatly around the

fish-man's throat, holding it tight
against the soft, shiny skin.

"Have *you* had enough?" he asked,
echoing the pirate's words.

The man let out a snorting chuckle.
"Aye!" he said at last. "You've got me
fair and square. I yield."

"So you'll show me where to
find sanguin root?" Tom asked, not
moving his sword.

"Aye," the pirate said again. Tom
took his sword from the piranha's
neck, and put it back into his
scabbard. He picked up his shield
and put it back over his shoulder.
The pirate turned, eyeing Tom with
grudging respect. Then he jerked his
head sideways. "Through there," he

said, turning to push between two
palm trees.

   Tom followed the pirate into a
shady grove, dappled with sunlight.
Growing from the moss in the
shadow of a lush green bush, Tom
spotted a cluster of red, heart-shaped

leaves. *Sanguin root!* Tom used the point of his sword to prise the plant, roots and all, from the loamy soil.

"Thank you!" he said, turning to the three pirates, who now stood side by side, blocking his exit from the grove. Tom started to push past them, but one of the smaller fish-men caught his shoulder. Tom turned angrily, impatience flooding his veins as he thought of Elenna waiting.

"I beat you!" Tom said. "Let me go!"

"But you've got to take all the spoils!" the man said.

"Yeah!" the fish-man with the peg leg chimed in. "These are yours now!" He thrust two red sticks of dynamite towards Tom. "Pirate's honour!"

Tom looked uneasily from the pirate, who was grinding his sharp teeth in agitation, to the lethal dynamite clutched in the man's scaled fist. Finally, Tom sighed. It didn't look like he had much choice.

"All right," Tom said, taking the dynamite. The pirate sagged with relief. Then the three fish-men each dipped Tom a sharp nod of approval and trudged away through the forest.

Tom tucked the dynamite into his belt, and, clutching his sanguin root, raced back through the trees to the beach.

He found Elenna as he had left her, slumped in the sand, but now the branching black veins had climbed her arm and were poking from her collar, reaching up the side of her neck. His heart gave a sickening jolt. He couldn't see her breathing at all.

Am I too late?

6

A RISKY PLAN

Tom watched Elenna's still, silent chest, willing it to move. Finally, he saw the shallowest lift of her ribs. *She* is *breathing!*

He fell to his knees at her side and ripped a handful of straggly roots from the plant in his hand. He shook away the soil and placed the roots on the rock, then pounded

them with a stone until blood-red
juice ran free. Tom pushed some
of the red pulp between Elenna's
blue-tinged lips. Still she didn't
move. Panic clutched Tom's heart,
but he wasn't ready to give up. He
massaged his friend's slack jaw,
working at the root with her teeth.
A moment later, she coughed and
shot upright, wide-eyed and staring.
She looked at her arm. The ugly
black lines faded to pale blue before
Tom's eyes. He grinned with relief.
The poison was gone! Elenna met
his smile with one of her own.

"You did it!" she said. Then
she glanced towards the flat,
clear water beyond the cove, and

shivered. "But we'll have to face Soara again. We can't let Amelia win."

Tom nodded, his relief at Elenna's recovery fading and worry creeping back. "You're right," he said. "Amelia would make a disastrous Mistress of the Beasts. She thinks everything's about fighting and glory. She has no idea—" Tom broke off. Floating in the glassy shallows near the shore, he could see a strip of grey wood with flaking white paint.

Their dinghy... Or part of it. Dread and guilt washed over him. He pushed the remains of the sanguin root deep into his pocket and hurried towards the

boat with Elenna at his side. When
they reached the shore, Tom saw
splintered wood where a terrible
blow had smashed the dinghy in

half, but there was no sign of the rest of the boat. An image of the sailing ship, trapped deep inside Soara's transparent body, flashed through Tom's mind, and he shuddered.

Elenna stared solemnly at the remains of the dinghy, then shook her head with a troubled frown. "Do you think the Beast ate Amelia and Dray?" she said.

"I hope not," Tom said. "But there's only one way to find out. We have to defeat Soara. And we won't do it out at sea. She's too powerful. We have to lure her into our territory… And I have an idea how."

It didn't take long for Tom to explain his plan to Elenna. He left her on the beach with his dynamite and instructions to build a fire, then waded into the sea. Moments later, Tom lay belly-up in the icy water of the inlet. He paddled gently with his hands, barely keeping his head above the surface, the weight of the shield on his back tugging him down. He had considered leaving his shield on the beach with Elenna, but now, out in the open, with the strange purple sky arching above him, he felt grateful for any protection it might offer against the Beast.

I'm going to use myself as bait for

*a giant jellyfish with deadly poison
and a sucking whirlpool gut,* he
thought. *This might be my craziest
plan yet!*

He tipped his head up slightly,
glancing over the water of the bay,
looking for any sign of Soara. His
gaze locked on a faint circle of
ripples in the distance. A translucent

lump broke the surface, gleaming with a purplish sheen in the light from the strange sky. Tom's breath caught in his throat. His pulse quickened, and he clenched his jaw, forcing himself to stay still, not to panic.

The vast jellyfish glided closer, long ripples streaming behind it. Soon Tom could feel the water around him moving, small waves breaking against him, lapping over his face. Still he didn't move. Each time he dared to glance up, Soara was closer, bigger, moving faster. Finally, when the fishy stink of the Beast filled his nostrils and the vast bulk of her body was almost on him,

Tom burst into action. He flipped onto his belly and swam towards the shore. Immediately, the sea around him bubbled. Rushing, sucking, slurping sounds filled his ears, and a strong tide tugged at his body.

It's working! She's following me, Tom realised. *Now all I have to do is stay alive!* But every stroke he made, and every kick of his legs, seemed harder and more sluggish against the strengthening current. The sucks and slurps from Soara's flesh behind him made his skin creep with fear and revulsion.

He pushed himself to swim harder and faster, his lungs burning, his arms windmilling through the water.

He longed for the power of the golden breastplate, but knew he was on his own. He focused on Elenna's form standing on the shore, beside her bright fire.

"Hurry, Tom!" she cried, her eyes fixed on the monster behind him.

Tom swam for his life, powering

towards his friend. Then the terrible force clutched at his foot, wrenching his leg as he tried to swim. *She's got me!* Tom kicked and struggled against the tentacle wrapped about his ankle, but his head sank beneath the surface. He twisted his body to see the swirling whirlpool in the

creature's flesh widening. Horror struck him to the core. Deep within Soara's body, he could see a familiar grey face. *Dray!* The giant man's eyes were closed. His body was perfectly still.

1

7

DESPERATE MEASURES

Terror gripped Tom's heart and, for a second or two, he felt paralysed.

The man had fought against them, but he had fought without fear. And now he was dead.

I don't plan on following him!

Tom drew his sword and hacked at the tentacle that held him. The water slowed the blade and the blow was feeble. Tom drew the blade back again, and this time stabbed deep into the slimy flesh. He felt the pressure about his ankle slacken, and twisted the blade. With a sucking pop, the tentacle unwound and rippled away. Tom turned and swam again, angling up towards the glistening surface.

He broke out under the purple sky, snatched a breath of air, then sheathed his sword.

Soara won't stay distracted for long...

He kicked his tired legs and clawed through the water away from the Beast.

Tom's lungs and muscles burned, but desperation gave him strength. He expected to feel more tentacles snag him at any second, ready to tug him under. But finally the seabed started to bank steeply upwards. He risked a look back, and saw the tell-tale swirls of water twenty paces away where Soara stirred. *I'm going to make it!* He glanced up to the beach, looking for Elenna.

His heart skipped a beat.

No!

Beside her fire, Elenna was on her knees, struggling to breathe. Amelia stood behind her, dripping with water, an arm looped around Elenna's throat.

At the sight of his friend helpless
in Amelia's grip, Tom's fear gave
way to rage. Elenna's bow and
arrow lay beside the fire she
had built, along with the two red

sticks of dynamite.

Amelia's going to get us all killed! What's she doing?

Tom lifted his head, treading water. "Amelia!" he shouted. "Let Elenna go! This isn't going to help any of us complete the Quest." Even from this distance, and with the splash of the Beast drawing closer behind him, Tom saw Amelia give a familiar proud hitch of her chin.

"You don't think so?" she called back. "Soara will be much easier to defeat if she's all tired out from overeating!"

Tom could hardly believe what he was hearing. Amelia's own uncle had been swallowed by the Beast.

Did she care about no one at all?

"I don't believe you're really descended from Kara," Tom cried, his feet finding the seabed. He began to stride from the water, reaching for his sword. "She fought with honour, while you—" *Smack!* Tom felt a powerful blow from Soara's tentacle lash across the shield on his back, driving him face-first below the waves. He came up gasping, winded, sucking burning water into his lungs. Instinct took control and he thrashed, managing to turn onto his back, his mouth and nose just clearing the surface. He coughed violently, spewing the water from his lungs. His throat burned. He tried to suck in a breath but his chest wouldn't move. A new wave of panic crashed over him as he registered an immense pressure tightening about his ribs, making them crack with a sickening pain. He lifted his head to see Soara's stringy tentacle wrapped about his chest.

"Still fighting, Tom?" cried Amelia. "Just give up! Only I shall return to Avantia!"

Tom tried to sink his fingers into the jellyfish's tentacle, but the limb was as hard as rubber as it squeezed tighter. He fumbled for his sword hilt, but the tentacle had coiled over it, trapping it against his side. It

shook him from side to side in the water.

"Help me!" he roared to the beach.

"Don't worry," Amelia crowed. "I'll tell them their hero died bravely."

"Oh, shut *up!*" shouted Elenna. With a grunt, she thrust an elbow into Amelia's gut, bending her double. Then she turned and tripped Amelia onto the sand. "Hold on, Tom!" she cried.

He saw her stoop to snatch up a stick of dynamite from the sand, then the tentacle yanked him under. He didn't even have time to take a breath this time, and the burn

across his chest was unbearable.
Panic drained any will to fight, as
red blobs rose up before his eyes.

It's over, he thought. *I've failed.*

BOOM! A current slammed into

him, tearing the tentacle from his body and throwing him hard into the seabed. Bubbles everywhere, the sea turned white. His body tumbled over and over. Finally, mercifully, everything went black.

THE NEXT QUEST

"Tom? Are you all right?" Elenna asked, her voice almost drowned out by the ringing in Tom's ears.

He sat up, and tried to speak, but a terrible pressure in his chest bent him double, racked by hacking wet coughs.

"I'm fine," he croaked, once he'd spewed all the water from his lungs.

"Thanks to your dynamite."

Foaming water rushed over his legs, tugging at his trousers and at the cold, wet sand beneath him. He glanced out over the bay. The wide inlet was scattered with debris, broken beams and tattered rags – Tom even spotted the hollow-eyed stare of a skull – but there was no sign of the Beast. Or Amelia. But then he spotted something that filled him with horror.

A long, grey body was floating face-down in the water, not far from the shore.

"Dray!" Tom cried. Together, he and Elenna waded out into the sea, towards the floating figure.

"Ah!" Elenna jumped. Powering towards them through the water, Tom spotted the bright red eyes and scaly face of a piranha pirate – the leader Tom had beat in a cutlass fight. The pirate's head broke the surface right beside Dray.

"What are you still doing here?" he barked. "You should leave while you can. And you can take this corpse with you." The pirate grabbed Dray's shoulder, and started tugging him towards the shore.

Tom took hold of Dray's other arm, shuddering at the cold, clammy touch of the big man's skin. "Don't worry," Tom told the pirate. "We're going, just as soon as we've done what we can for our...friend." Heavy dread weighed Tom down as he thought how little that might be. *A shallow grave on the beach?*

When they reached the shore, Tom and the pirate laid Dray down on his back. Any hope Tom had that Amelia's uncle might somehow be alive faded away. Dray's face showed no sign of life at all. Elenna dropped to the tall man's side and put a hand on his chest, her expression grave as she checked for a heartbeat. She shook her head. "He's gone, Tom."

The pirate chuckled mirthlessly. "He won't be the first who drowned in these waters."

Tom wondered what this meant for the Quest. Perhaps Amelia would decide to give up and go home. *If that's even possible...*

Elenna snatched her hand back suddenly and let out a yelp of surprise as Dray stirred.

"Sorcery!" cried the piranha man.

Dray sat bolt upright and gazed about, a faint frown of confusion creasing his forehead. Tom gasped, staring closely at him. *There's no way he can be alive.*

He glanced at Elenna, and they shared a wide-eyed look of alarm.

"Thank you for saving my uncle!" Amelia's voice rang out heartily behind them. Tom turned sharply

to see her limping over the sand,
grimacing in pain with each step.

A growl rumbled from the piranha
pirate's throat. "More intruders!"

he said, glowering sideways at Tom. "We made a pirate's deal with you and your friend, not that other girl and this big lump. They must leave Corsair Island. Now. I'll give them to the count of ten to shift. After that…" The pirate drew his fingers expressively across his bulging throat.

Amelia scowled at the pirate, her dark eyes narrowed with disgust and her hand tight on the shaft of her axe. "You and whose army?" she said, squaring her shoulders. The pirate stepped before her and drew himself up tall, then he craned forwards and snapped his pointed teeth. Amelia edged back, her face

as grey as the sand. Tom had to
stifle a smile as he stepped between
Amelia and the fish-man.

"We're going now anyway," Tom
said. "Our passage to the next stage
of the trial awaits us." Tom pointed
towards the water's edge. The pirate
frowned and followed the line of
Tom's finger.

An eddy swirled in the shallows,
near to where they were standing,
but instead of it being crystal clear,
the water at the whirlpool's heart
was a black so complete it looked
like a hole in the world – which, in
a way, it was. The pirate's fishy jaws
spread into a knowing grin.

"It's the portal to the next

Quest!" Elenna said.

Dray turned to gaze at the swirling darkness before them. The piranha pirate stepped behind him. "A big oaf too dim to know when he's been eaten by a jellyfish has no place on Corsair Island," he said. "Off you go!" The pirate shoved Dray hard towards the inky pool. The giant man toppled, and disappeared into its depths.

"Hey, that's my uncle!" cried Amelia.

The pirate gave a nod to the treeline, and two of his crew strode out from the tress. One wrapped his arms around Amelia's waist, the other grabbed her feet. "Let

me go!" Amelia shouted, but the
pirates hoisted her across the sand
like a sack of grain. She screamed
in rage, flailing like a fish, but
just looked like a toddler having
a tantrum. The fish-men carried
her effortlessly to the portal, then
chucked her through. Tom caught

one last glimpse of Amelia's furious face before she vanished into darkness. The piranha pirates dusted off their hands, then their leader turned to Tom and Elenna with a broad, toothy grin. "Nothing but hot air, that one," he said. "In fact, I'd say she's more full of wind than Chomper's guts after a plate of beans. Now, I wish you luck on your Quest." He lifted his hand in a quick salute, then turned and trudged away up the beach.

Elenna's eyes glittered as she watched the fish-man go. "We'd better hurry. Goodness knows what Amelia will get up to if we give her a head start."

"You're right," Tom said. *Another trial awaits!*

He turned towards the black depths of the portal in the shallows. Compared to the grey and purple landscape around him, it looked strangely inviting.

He and Elenna clasped hands, and then jumped together.

THE END

CONGRATULATIONS, YOU HAVE COMPLETED THIS QUEST!

At the end of each chapter you were awarded a special gold coin.
The QUEST in this book was worth an amazing 8 coins.

Look at the Beast Quest totem picture inside the back cover of this book to see how far you've come in your journey to become

MASTER OF THE BEASTS.

The more books you read, the more coins you will collect!

Do you want your own
Beast Quest Totem?

1. Cut out and collect the coin below
2. Go to the Beast Quest website
3. Download and print out your totem
4. Add your coin to the totem
www.beastquest.co.uk/totem

Don't miss the next exciting Beast Quest book, DROGAN THE JUNGLE MENACE!

Read on for a sneak peek...

AN UNEASY ALLIANCE

Rushing water swirled around Tom as the whirlpool dragged him down.

Can't breathe! Drowning!

He tumbled through the churning water, the weight of his sword and shield pulling him deeper. Without the power of his Golden Armour he couldn't fight the deadly current.

He kicked hard, trying to push upwards, or what he thought was upwards. His chest ached painfully, as though an iron clamp were being tightened around his ribs.

Must reach the surface!

Through a flurry of bubbles, he saw Elenna's terrified face, her eyes wide with panic as she fought the savage flood.

Lights burst behind Tom's eyes. The agony in his chest was excruciating. He could feel the strength draining from his muscles. His lungs were screaming.

In moments, he would be dead.

Suddenly, the sucking sensation was gone. Gritting his teeth, he ploughed upwards, snatching at Elenna's arm and towing her along.

He saw sunbeams dancing on the surface above him. A silent cry escaped his mouth.

At last, his head burst from the water and he sucked in air. *Made it…*

He heard Elenna coughing at his side. "I thought we weren't going to escape," she said, panting.

"Me, too," Tom admitted. As he recovered, he glanced around. He'd half expected to see the ocean again, where they'd battled Soara the Stinging Spectre, but instead he found himself in the middle of a swamp. Dirty water led to mangrove forests on all sides.

The black portal had transported

them to a new destination – some sort of humid jungle.

Tom struck out with Elenna through the choppy water towards a narrow, boggy shore, and soon his feet sank into soft mud under him. He floundered towards dry land. Elenna waded through the brown water at his side.

The air was heavy and sticky, and strange insects buzzed and flitted over the water's edge.

"You didn't drown, then," said a sarcastic voice. "I'm so very pleased about that."

Tom and Elenna clambered out of the shallows. Amelia and her uncle, Dray, were standing just under the canopy of trees. Dray was tall and bald, with greyish skin and a grim, unreadable face. Amelia was a few years older than Tom and Elenna, with long blonde hair and mocking blue eyes. It was she who had spoken. She was looking at her map, and neither of them made any attempt to help Tom and Elenna out of the clinging mud.

Tom gave Amelia a hard look, trying to swallow his anger. "We've all been lucky so far," he said. "But unless we start working together, I won't be able to protect you."

Amelia smirked. "What makes you think I need your protection?"

"Let's just stop squabbling,"

Elenna said, with a sigh.

"I agree," said Amelia. "We can stop it right now if you two give up and go home." She gave Tom a superior look. "You know I'm the true Mistress of the Beasts. I'm going to complete the Trial of Heroes and claim the Golden Armour. It's inevitable – my birth right."

Tom seethed with anger and frustration, taking out his own map, which must have been made from magical parchment because it was completely dry. Amelia had shown up at King Hugo's palace in Avantia, claiming to be the direct descendant of a past Mistress of the Beasts named Kara the Fearless.

Despite all the Quests that Tom had
undergone, Amelia insisted that she
was the true protector of Avantia.
The former wizard, Aduro, had

consulted the ancient chronicles and had ruled that the two candidates had to undergo the Trial of Heroes to discover which one was worthy. It was the custom when there were competing claims.

I need to get to that axe first, Tom thought, as he scanned the map. It showed miles of jungle without end, but right in the centre flashed a red dot. Beneath it was written a name – *DROGAN*.

The next Beast...

Elenna pointed at Amelia. "You talk about going home," she said. "But where *is* your home? Where were you hiding all those years while Tom and I have been keeping

Avantia and the other realms safe?"

A red flush burned across Amelia's face. "My home is a village near the Northern Mountains," she said sharply. "My parents died when I was a child – but a wise man recognised that I was a descendent of Mistress Kara and taught me about my heritage."

Tom felt some sympathy at hearing Amelia's tale. He'd lost his father too, and had never seen his mother, Freya, when he was growing up. "We come from similar backgrounds," he said. "That's all the more reason to work together – destiny will decide who is the true Master of the Beasts."

"Mistress of the Beasts," Amelia

interrupted. "And destiny needs a push every now and then." Her eyes flashed. "I deserve to win."

"You're selfish and unworthy," snapped Tom. "If not for your uncle, you would already be dead."

"And exactly who is this man you call your uncle?" exclaimed Elenna. "He was sucked into Soara's belly." Tom recalled the horrible moment clearly – they'd all thought Dray was dead. "He was underwater so long he should have drowned," Elenna continued. "How is he even alive?"

Amelia waved a dismissive hand. "My uncle is…very tough," she said.

"That's one word for it," said Elenna, eyeing Dray warily. As usual, the big brute didn't say a word.

Amelia snarled at her. "Just keep out of our way from now on, or I won't be held responsible for your fate! Come on, Uncle."

She turned and strode away under the trees. With a single, grim look at Tom and Elenna, Dray walked past her, ripping his way through the vegetation as though the leaves and ferns were no tougher than cobwebs. The jungle quickly swallowed them both.

Read
DROGAN THE JUNGLE MENACE
to find out what happens next!

Discover the new Beast Quest mobile game from

▶ PLAY GAMES

Available free on iOS and Android

Guide Tom on his Quest to free the Good Beasts
of Avantia from Malvel's evil spells.

Battle the Beasts, defeat the minions,
unearth the secrets and collect
rewards as you journey through the
Kingdom of Avantia.

DOWNLOAD THE APP TO BEGIN
THE ADVENTURE NOW!